2/15

Persian Cats

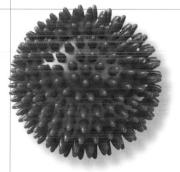

BY TAMMY GAGNE

The Child's World®

Published by The Child's World®
1980 Lookout Drive • Mankato, MN 56003-1705
800-599-READ • www.childsworld.com

Acknowledgments
The Child's World®: Mary Berendes, Publishing Director
Red Line Editorial: Editorial direction
The Design Lab: Design
Amnet: Production
Design elements: iStockphoto; Richard Peterson/Shutterstock
Images; Africa Studio/Shutterstock Images; Willem Havenaar/
Shutterstock Images

Photographs ©: iStockphoto, cover, 1, 5, 6, 11, 15, 17, 20, 23;
Richard Peterson/Shutterstock Images, cover, 1; Africa Studio/
Shutterstock Images, cover, 1; Willem Havenaar/Shutterstock
Images, cover, 1; Public Domain, 9; Maria Dryfhout/Shutterstock
Images, 13; JJ Studio/Shutterstock Images, 19

ISBN 9781626873841
LCCN 2014930641

Printed in the United States of America
Mankato, MN
July, 2014
PA02226

ABOUT THE AUTHOR

Tammy Gagne has written dozens of books about the health and behavior of animals for both adults and children. Her most recent titles include Great Predators: Crocodiles *and* Super Smart Animals: Dolphins. *She lives in northern New England with her husband, son, and a menagerie of pets.*

CONTENTS

Fit for Royalty

People have loved Persian cats since Great Britain's Victorian era in the 1800s. Rich, important people owned this beautiful **breed**. Some people owned more than one Persian. Even Queen Victoria owned this noble cat.

Persians stood out from other cat breeds from the very beginning. Their round heads, flat faces, and short bodies gave them a special look. Their long fur also drew attention.

Over the last two hundred years, breeders have created two types of Persians. Some Persians look more like their early **ancestors**. People call these cats **traditional** Persians. Most modern show cats have different features. Their faces are shorter and flatter than early members of the breed.

Some people worry about one health problem modern Persians suffer from. Many show cats have problems breathing. This is because they have short noses.

The Traditional Cat Association has a separate name for traditional Persians. It calls them Doll Face Persians.

Both types of Persians have sweet personalities. The breed is well known for this feature. It is one of the biggest reasons Persians are one of the most popular cat breeds throughout the world.

Persians have gained popularity over the years for their looks and sweet personalities.

Older than History

The Persian cat breed has been around for hundreds of years. The very first cat shows in the 1870s in Great Britain included Persians. There are no paper records of the breed before that time. But one could say its history was written in stone instead. Hieroglyphics of a cat that looks like the Persian have been found in Iran. This is the modern name for the area once known as Persia. This is where Persian cats are thought to have come from.

The first Europeans to discover this longhaired breed were diplomats. They traveled for work. Many of these travelers brought cats home with them in the mid-1800s. The cats were from Middle Eastern countries. People in Great Britain, France, and Italy fell in love with the Persian instantly. Its loving personality was an important reason to like this cat.

The Persian's coat is the longest of any cat breed.

Persians' long, beautiful coats are one of the features people have been noticing for hundreds of years.

Developing the Breed

As soon as the Europeans discovered Persians, they began breeding the cats themselves. They also crossed Persians with other Middle Eastern cat breeds. Many Persians were bred with Angoras. This cat breed was from Turkey. It had a finer, silkier coat than a Persian. Its hair was also longer than a Persian's coat. The breeds shared many traits. But they were also different from one another.

Breeders did not focus on keeping the Angora breed going. It was thought to have died out. But it was rediscovered in Turkey in 1962.

The American public first saw Persians in 1895. A show at Madison Square Garden in New York City included the exotic breed. Many of the cats in that show were white Persians. This color was a feature that had come from crossing the breed with Angoras.

Many cat breeds suffered as a result of World War I and World War II. Breeding cats became less common during these

difficult times. Some breeds nearly died out. The Persian's popularity helped it survive. Many people wanted one of these cats. This kept the Persian breed alive.

Persians and Angoras were often bred together in the late 1800s.

Furry and Fabulous

The Persian's long, flowing coat makes it look noble. Many people want to reach out and pet Persians when they see them. The fur is soft on most cats. It is not just the long hair that gives this breed its special appearance, however.

Persians are known as much for their shape as for their coat. Nearly everything about this breed is short and **stocky**. The head is round. The body is square with short legs. They also have a short, thick tail.

Persians have a much flatter face than other cats. Many people compare this breed's face to a pansy. Its round eyes remind many people of this popular flower. The eyes on most Persians are a bright shade of copper.

Some solid white Persians have one blue and one copper-colored eye.

A few Persians have blue, green, or greenish-blue eyes, rather than copper-colored.

Pick a Color

Persians come in more than 80 different colors and patterns. Professionally, the breed is shown in seven different divisions. Each one is based on the cat's color.

The most common solid colors are white, black, and cream. The breed also comes in chocolate and lilac. But these colors are quite rare.

Shaded and chinchilla Persians have a solid base color. They also have dark-tipped hairs. The smoke Persian looks like a solid-colored cat. But when taking a closer look, one can see this cat has six different colors. Persians may also have a **tabby** coloring. Some Persians have colors that mix together. Other Persians have just two colors on their coats.

The Himalayan Persian looks a lot like a Siamese cat. This color variety was made from breeding Persians with Siamese cats.

Himalayan Persians have the colors of a Siamese but the body and coat of a Persian.

Calm and Confident

The Persian is a good fit for many different households. This is not a cat that gets into mischief or demands attention. It enjoys doing its own thing.

Persians are good choices for families with kids. These cats enjoy being petted or brushed. A Persian cat may chase a ball a short distance. But Persians do not like to play for a long time.

Persian cats will not climb onto tall furniture. They do not like jumping. Persians enjoy being lap cats. A Persian may greet its owner when he or she returns home. But it will occupy itself until then.

Many cats use their voices to get attention. Owners will enjoy hearing this breed's soft meows. This does not happen often.

Most Persians live happily in the same homes with other cats or dogs.

Persian cats may enjoy batting at a feather toy.

Attention, Please

Some people believe Persians are cats that do not care about things. This is not true. Persians are okay being alone. Other cat breeds need more attention. Persians are happy to play alone. But they also enjoy spending time with their owners.

It takes time for a Persian to bond with its favorite people. But once a person earns this cat's love, regular attention is welcomed.

If a favorite person ignores this cat, he or she will see a more demanding side of the Persian. This cat will beg for attention. A head scratch will fix the problem.

Hermione Grainger's cat Crookshanks from the *Harry Potter* book and movie series is a Persian.

Many Persians are happy to sit near their favorite humans.

Low Energy, Not No Energy

If you want a cat that likes to cuddle, life with a Persian is great. It takes a while for a kitten to relax, though. They must grow into this. Persian kittens are playful and mischievous like other breeds.

Even though Persians are calm, they still like play time. Running after toys is good exercise. It is an easy way to get your Persian to exercise.

Persians are very smart cats. If they need or want something, they will get your attention. It is important to give them your attention. They may be trying to tell you something. Persians will give up if you do not respond to them.

Because of its long coat, the Persian is not meant to be an outdoor cat.

A Persian will not play with toys as long as many other breeds.

It is important to groom your Persian cat to prevent its long coat from matting.

A Bathing Beauty

Regular **grooming** is important for Persians. They need regular brushing and combing. Their long, thick coats can become matted very quickly.

Baths are also important to keep this longhaired breed clean. Brushing must come first, however. A matted coat that is wet will become almost impossible to untangle with a brush or comb. If this happens, the Persian may need to have some fur shaved off.

Cats in general are known for disliking water. But Persians usually don't mind being bathed. The trick is bathing when a kitten is young. It will think baths are normal. Then it will not be afraid of baths as it gets older.

Some owners opt to cut their Persian's hair. Clipped cats cannot be in cat shows. But once the hair grows out, they look no different than other Persians.

Like other breeds, Persians need to eat a healthy diet. Owners must also take them to the veterinarian. A Persian can live from 15 to 20 years when well cared for.

Glossary

ancestors (AN-sess-turs) Ancestors are those from whom a species is descended. Traditional Persians look like their ancestors.

breed (BREED) A breed is a group of animals that are different from related members of its species. The Persian is a popular cat breed.

diplomats (DIP-luh-mats) Diplomats are people employed by a country to work with other countries. European diplomats were the first owners of Persian cats.

divisions (di-VIZH-uhns) Divisions are parts that make up a whole. Persians have seven different divisions in cat shows.

exotic (eg-ZOT-ik) Exotic is something introduced from another country. The Persian was an exotic breed at the first New York cat show.

grooming (GROOM-ing) Grooming is cleaning and keeping up the appearance. Grooming is an important piece of taking care of your cat.

hieroglyphics (hye-ur-uh-GLIF-iks) Hieroglyphics are writing that is made up of pictures and symbols instead of words. Some hieroglyphics had cats that looked like Persians.

stocky (STOK-ee) To be stocky is to be sturdy and thick in build. Persians have a stocky build.

tabby (TAB-ee) A tabby cat has a striped or spotted coat. Some Persians have a tabby coat.

traditional (truh-DISH-uhn-uhl) Traditional is based on custom. Traditional Persians look like their ancestors.

To Learn More

BOOKS

Bailey, Gwen. *What Is My Cat Thinking?* San Diego: Thunder Bay Press, 2010.

Gagne, Tammy. *Amazing Cat Facts and Trivia.* New York: Chartwell Books, 2011.

WEB SITES

Visit our Web site for links about Persian cats:
www.childsworld.com/links

Note to Parents, Teachers, and Librarians: We routinely verify our Web links to make sure they are safe and active sites. So encourage your readers to check them out!

23

Index